D1107364

MY CLEMENTINE

ROBERTO INNOCENTI

CREATIVE EDITIONS

THIS IS MY SHIP. She is sinking.

We've seen the world, this old girl and I.

They say the captain goes down with his ship. But this is one journey I won't be making with her. Not yet.

This is our story.

When I was a boy, I dreamed of the sea.
I told the laundress's daughter I'd be captain
one day. *You'll see.*

I was there when my ship was built. From bow to stern, she was beautiful.

Clementine was her name.

She was my destiny.

We launched from San Francisco as the sun rose.

I was young. I was green.

And when Clementine set off to sea,
I was home.

We ventured to faraway ports with pretty names—Pago Pago, Papeete, Panama.

We filled Clementine's hull with fresh fruit.

Flocks of gulls and porpoise pods followed in our wake.

Unfamiliar flags would meet us.

Familiar faces would greet us.

 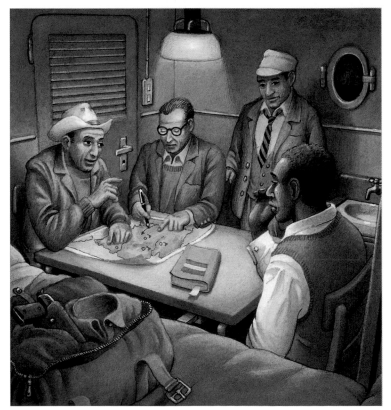

Every day at sea was an adventure.

Fighters from friendly lands. Adversaries on distant horizons.

The days were long. The nights even longer.

Where would we be tomorrow?   Cartagena, Havana, Valencia.

Lisbon, Bordeaux, Liverpool.

One day, the captain asked me if I wanted to take the helm. It was time. The sea was changing.

So was the world around us.

After so many peaceful days at sea, a war had caught up with us.

Clementine was called to serve.

My little cargo ship was now a warship.

From bright tropical waters, we found ourselves in bitter polar seas.
Luckily, we had an ally to break the ice.

And Clementine to take care of us.   Through war and peace.

Time moves more slowly on the sea.
Still, the years, like faraway ports, passed by.
Suva, Surabaya, Salvador.

Alice's letters always found me.

We've seen the world, Clementine and I.

Our last voyage together began like any other.

But it ended with us going our separate ways.
It was time to let Clementine go.

Before she sank, Clementine made sure her
captain and crew were safe.
And then she went down.

And I went home.
Alice was waiting for me.

And my Clementine?

She's in the one place she'd never been . . .

The bottom of the sea.

MY CLEMENTINE tells the story of a fictional ship's extraordinary 50-year life—from the early 1930s, when Clementine was built and launched, to her travels around the world, through her service in war and peace, to her eventual resting place at the bottom of the sea.

Clementine was a refrigerated cargo ship, or "reefer." Reefers transport perishable goods such as fruit, fish, meat, vegetables, and dairy products that require temperature-controlled conditions. The holds of old reefer ships were cooled by large blocks of ice, which were loaded upon departure from a port. Modern reefers, like Clementine, are equipped with refrigerators instead.

More than 300 feet (91.4 m) long from bow to stern and 40 feet (12.2 m) wide from port to starboard, a ship like Clementine is also known as a "three island ship" because its three superstructures—forecastle, bridge, and poop—look like three islands when the lower part of the hull is below the horizon. Reefer ships are painted white to help keep them cool. During the second World War, reefer ships like Clementine were used by the United States Navy to transport soldiers and supplies to and from Europe. In peacetime, they were often returned to commercial use.

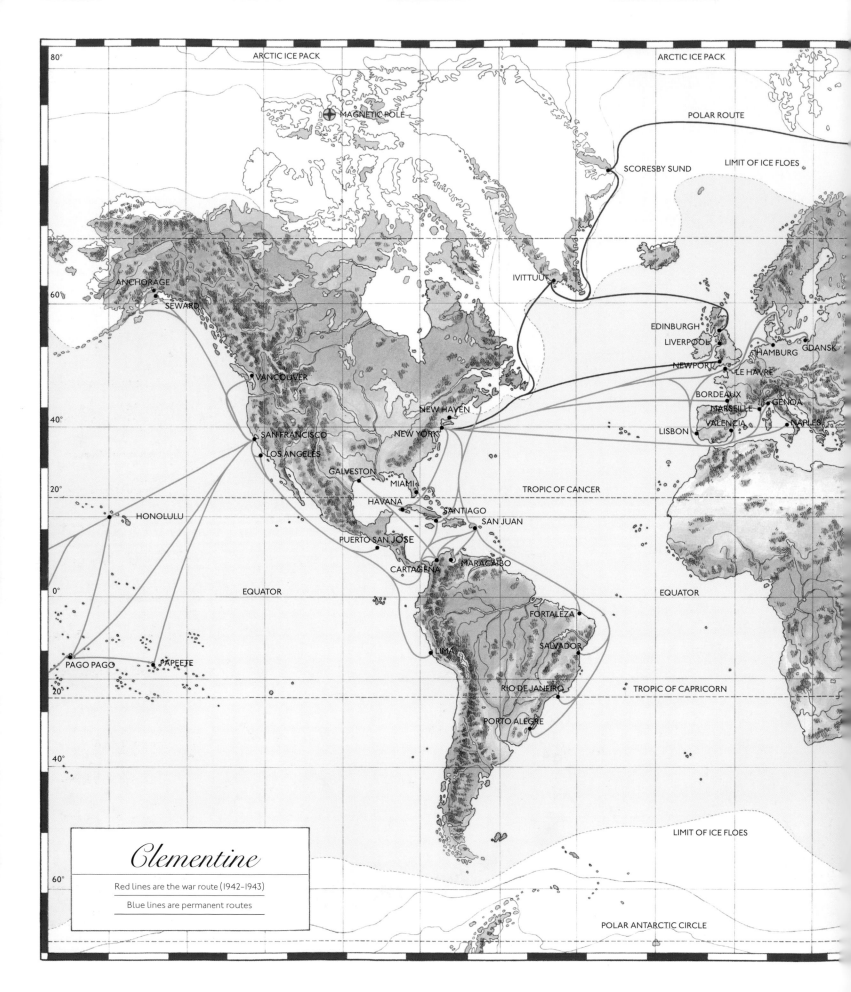

ARCTIC ICE PACK   ARCTIC ICE PACK

80°

MAGNETIC POLE

POLAR ROUTE

SCORESBY SUND   LIMIT OF ICE FLOES

60°

IVITTUUT

ANCHORAGE

SEWARD

EDINBURGH

LIVERPOOL   HAMBURG   GDANSK

NEWPORT   LE HAVRE

VANCOUVER

BORDEAUX

MARSEILLE   GENOA

40°   NEW HAVEN   VALENCIA   NAPLES

SAN FRANCISCO   NEW YORK   LISBON

LOS ANGELES

GALVESTON

MIAMI

20°   HAVANA   TROPIC OF CANCER

SANTIAGO

HONOLULU   SAN JUAN

PUERTO SAN JOSE

CARTAGENA   MARACAIBO

0°   EQUATOR   EQUATOR

FORTALEZA

LIMA   SALVADOR

PAGO PAGO   PAPEETE

20°   RIO DE JANEIRO   TROPIC OF CAPRICORN

PORTO ALEGRE

LIMIT OF ICE FLOES

Clementine

Red lines are the war route (1942–1943)

Blue lines are permanent routes

60°

POLAR ANTARCTIC CIRCLE

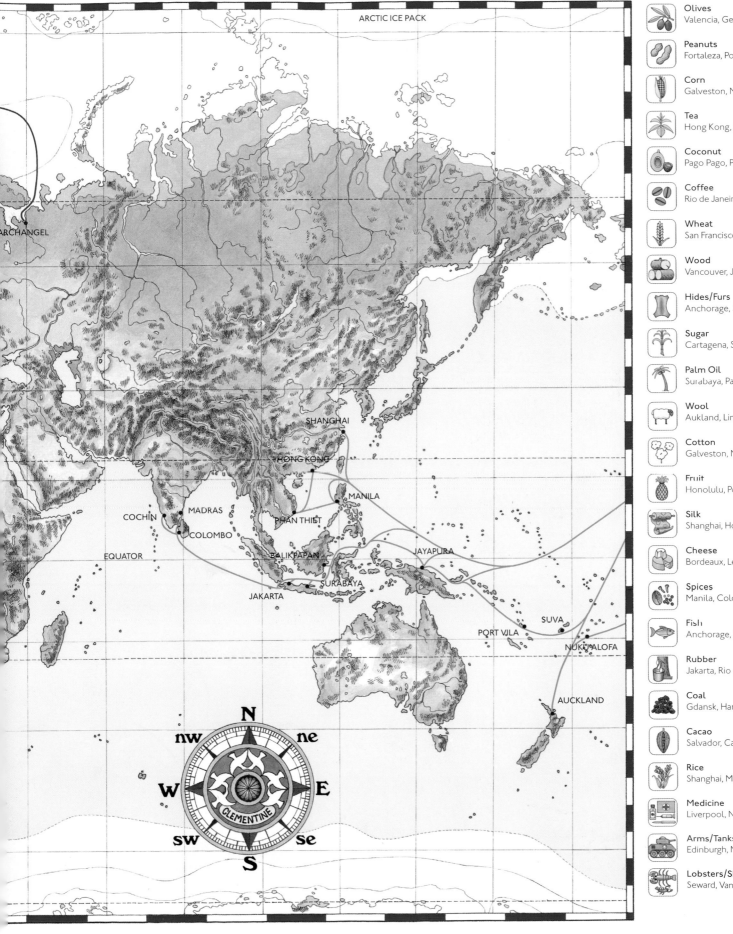

ARCTIC ICE PACK

ARCHANGEL

SHANGHAI

HONG KONG

MANILA

MADRAS
COCHIN
PHAN THIET
COLOMBO

EQUATOR

BALIKPAPAN
JAKARTA
SURABAYA

JAYAPURA

SUVA
PORT VILA
NUKU'ALOFA

AUCKLAND

N
nw   ne
W   **E**
sw   se
S
CLEMENTINE

Olives
Valencia, Genoa

Peanuts
Fortaleza, Porto Alegre, San Juan

Corn
Galveston, Miami, Vancouver

Tea
Hong Kong, Colombo, Madras

Coconut
Pago Pago, Papeete, Jayapura

Coffee
Rio de Janeiro, Maracaibo, Fortaleza

Wheat
San Francisco, Galveston, New York

Wood
Vancouver, Jakarta, Rio de Janeiro

Hides/Furs
Anchorage, Seward, Vancouver

Sugar
Cartagena, Santiago, Havana

Palm Oil
Surabaya, Pago Pago, Manila

Wool
Aukland, Lima, Liverpool

Cotton
Galveston, Madras, Miami

Fruit
Honolulu, Porto Alegre, Salvador

Silk
Shanghai, Hong Kong, Phan Thiet

Cheese
Bordeaux, Le Havre

Spices
Manila, Colombo, Balikpapan

Fish
Anchorage, Seward, Edinburgh

Rubber
Jakarta, Rio de Janeiro

Coal
Gdansk, Hamburg

Cacao
Salvador, Cartagena, Maracaibo

Rice
Shanghai, Madras, Cochin, Manila

Medicine
Liverpool, Newport, Archangel

Arms/Tanks
Edinburgh, Newport, Archangel

Lobsters/Shellfish
Seward, Vancouver, New Haven

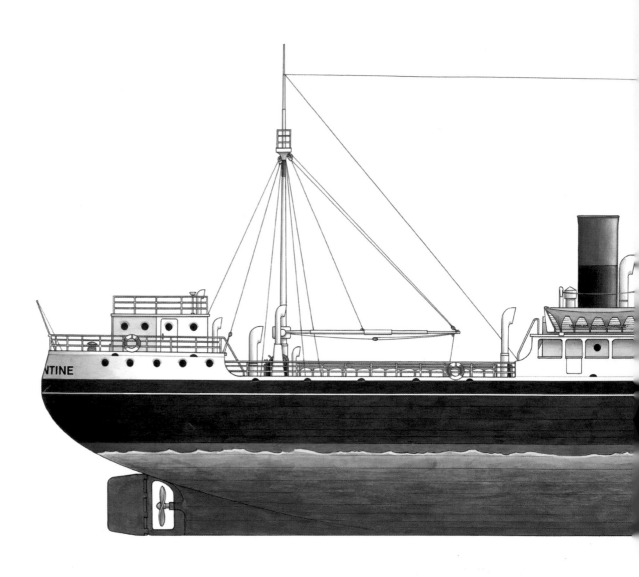

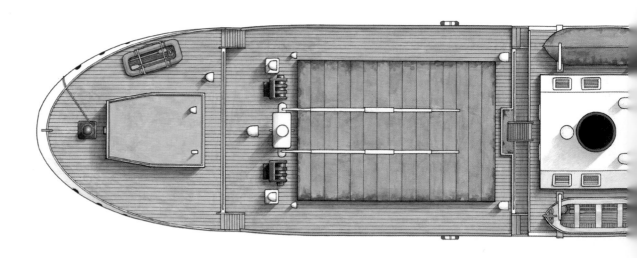

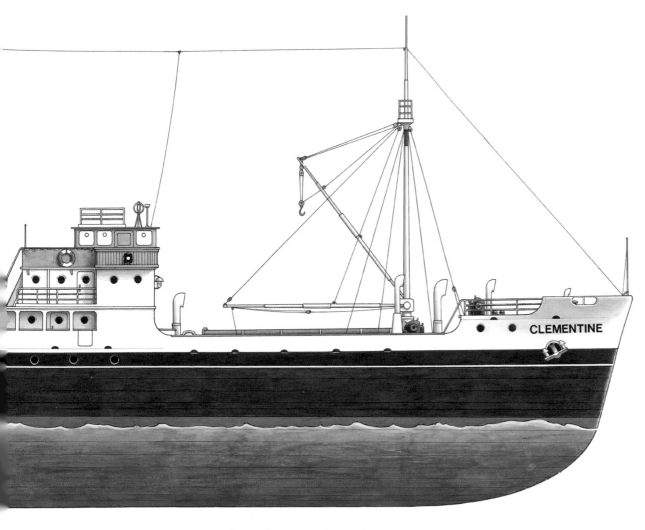

Clementine, from stern (back) to bow (front)

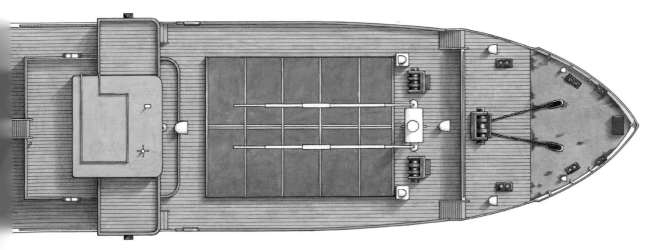

Clementine's port (left) and starboard (right) sides

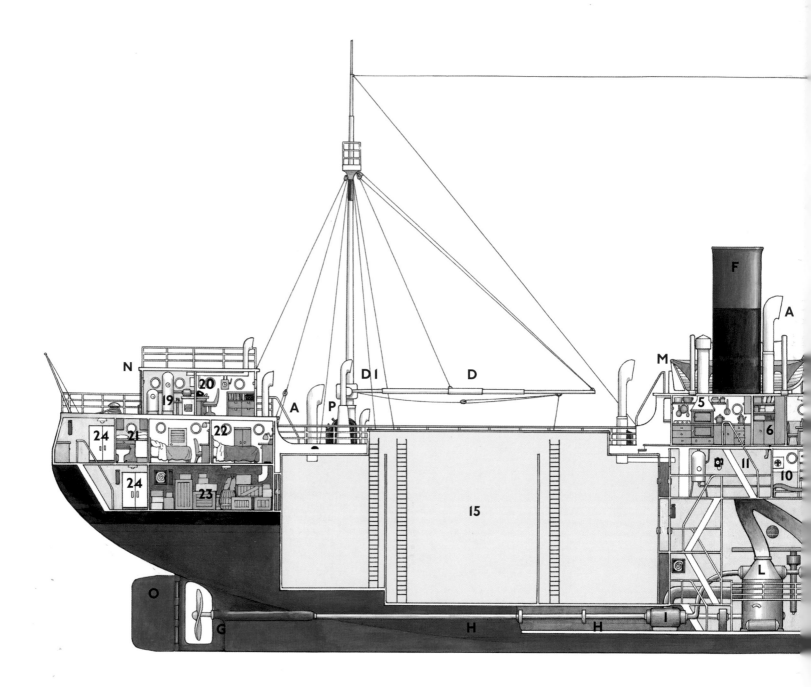

A	Air Intakes	H	Arbor Shaft	I	Chart Room	
B	Anchor Windlass	I	Generator		Steering Gear and Gyrocompass	
C	Anchor Slot	L	Engines	2	Captain's Cabin	
D	Thirty-Ton Cargo Boom	M	Life-Boat Deck	3	Officers' Accommodations	
D1	Mainmast	N	Poop Castle	4	Officers' Bathroom	
D2	Foremast	O	Rudder	5	Galley	
E	Radar Beacon	P	Cargo Winch	6	Storeroom	
F	Smokestack			7	Refectory	
G	Propeller			8	Radio Telegraph Room	

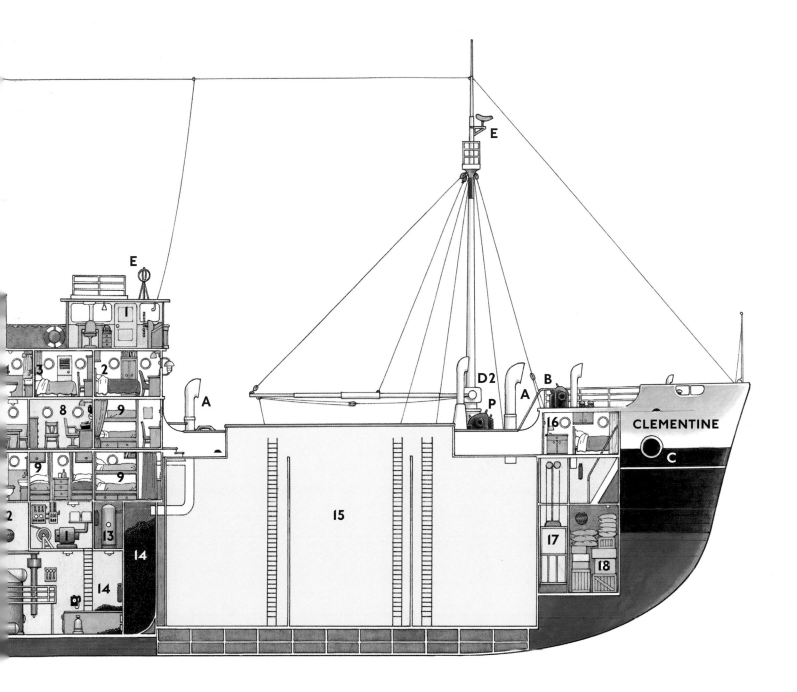

9	Two-Berth Cabin for Crew
10	Sickbay
11	Water Storage
12	Engine Room
13	Oil Storage
14	Coal Hold
15	Afterhold and Forehold (Refrigerated Hold)
16	Forecastle with Passengers' Accommodation
17	Elevator

18	Storehouse and Mail Service
19	Freshwater Storage
20	Office
21	Laundry/Bathroom
22	Poop with Passengers' Accommodation
23	Storehouse and Mail Service
24	Refrigerated Pantry

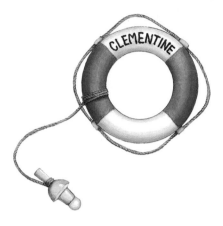

Text copyright © 2018 Creative Editions   Illustrations copyright © 2018 Roberto Innocenti

Edited by Amy Novesky   Designed by Rita Marshall

Published in 2018 by Creative Editions   P.O. Box 227, Mankato, MN 56002 USA

Creative Editions is an imprint of The Creative Company www.thecreativecompany.us

Printed in China

Library of Congress Cataloging-in-Publication Data

Names: Innocenti, Roberto, illustrator.

Title: My Clementine / by Roberto Innocenti.

Summary: A longtime captain of a refrigerated cargo ship named Clementine
narrates the many adventures of the ship, from its building
in the 1930s through the next five decades of travel.

Identifiers: LCCN 2017048935 / ISBN 978-1-56846-323-0

Subjects: CYAC: Ships—Fiction. / Seafaring life—Fiction. / Adventure and adventurers—Fiction.

Classification: LCC PZ7.1586 My 2018   DDC [E]—dc23

First edition 9 8 7 6 5 4 3 2 1